DOCTOR · WHO

DECIDE YOUR DESTINY

Dark Planet

by Davey Moore

Dark Planet

1 | 'Run!' shouts the Doctor. And so you run — really fast.

A few moments ago, you'd never even met this 'Doctor' — but now you're doing exactly what he says. It makes sense. The last person he told to run didn't go anywhere and... well, it was hard to see what exactly happened... he just seemed to get swallowed up by the approaching shadows.

So you do what the Doctor tells you and you run... towards a blue, wooden cabinet. White light pours through square windows around the top of the strange box, challenging the oncoming darkness. You're about to question the good sense of getting inside this cabinet when a girl pushes you through the door and then... well, something's not right because suddenly you're in a massive room.

It's like a scrapyard turned inside out. Or an antique shop from the future where everything is ancient yet advanced at the same time.

Your thoughts are interrupted as the girl tells you her name is Martha, that you are in something called the TARDIS and that the Doctor is going to get you to safety. You're still not sure what you're escaping from — just that, outside in the street, right in the middle of the day, it started to get very dark.

There's no time to take in any more because the Doctor is yelling at you. He is struggling to hold down a lever that seems to be trying to buck right out of his hands. He urges you to press a button. You ask him which one.

The Doctor shouts over the whine of some sort of engine, 'Just! Press! A! Button!' There are three buttons right in front of you: one red, one yellow and one green.

To hit the red button, turn to 29. To press the yellow button, turn to 51. To punch the green button, turn to 73.

Outside the church, you glance around nervously as the Doctor talks about eerie white insects squirming about in the crypt. Martha mentions a mysterious figure moving about and describes a strange scene in the stained glass. You all agree that it's time to find someone who might be able to tell you what's going on.

You walk downhill, stumbling over dry, dead grass. The Doctor wonders why it's so dark.

'It's night-time,' says Martha, plainly.

'But the TARDIS indicated it was 2pm,' says the Doctor.

You wonder if maybe there's an eclipse.

'Or a return to the Dark Ages,' quips Martha. You laugh, but the Doctor does not.

'Whatever's happening here, it's no joke,' says the Doctor. He thrusts an arm out in front of Martha — it hits her square in the chest and stops her dead in her tracks.

'Ooof,' says Martha. 'What are you...?' She trails off as she sees that the Doctor has just saved your lives!

In the darkness, you were about to stumble over the edge of a cliff, down to what looks like the sea. A very dead sea. You didn't realise you were near the sea because there's no breeze, no sound of the waves. In fact, there's no tide at all, just a yellowish foam where still, stagnant water meets slimy pebbles.

There's a strong and distinct tang in the air, like when your mum forgot about some vegetables and you found them rotting in the bottom drawer of the fridge.

'I wouldn't fancy a day out on that beach,' says Martha.

You find a path and follow it a short way along the cliff top. After a while, the path turns inland towards a rusty gate. You can just make out the familiar shape of a rollercoaster silhouetted against the flat, grey sky.

'Oooh, a funfair!' says the Doctor, brightly. 'That might cheer us up.'

To follow Martha to the hall of mirrors, turn to 89. To check out the ghost train with the Doctor, turn to 32.

3 As the Doctor strolls away to explore the environment, the monk-like figure introduces himself to you as Payton. He has a kind and gentle manner.

'I'm sorry if my appearance frightened you,' he says. You mention seeing him at the chapel and he says, 'Yes! I was leaving to meet Akemi and Teah. We meet at the old fairground — no one comes here.'

He explains that Akemi and Teah are romantically linked and hoping to marry. But they are in an impossible situation — they are from different Sides. You ask him what he means by 'Sides'.

'Teah is from the Down Side,' Payton patiently explains to you, 'where we are now. But Akemi lives up there.'

Payton points upwards. You ask him if he means up in the sky.

He laughs and says, 'No! On the Up Side!'

You want to ask more questions but you're distracted as the Doctor calls out to you.

Turn to 75.

4 Your legs wave in mid-air, hands aching as you cling to the ladder. Suddenly there's a rumbling. It sounds like... a rollercoaster!

You can't hold on any longer. You let go. You drop... and land in the seat of a moving carriage with the Doctor sitting in it. Oof!

'Perfect timing,' says the Doctor, waving his sonic screwdriver. 'I used this to loosen the wheels on this thing...' He clambers around on the outside of the trundling carriage and manages to bring it to a halt.

You're just getting your breath back when Payton comes sliding down the track behind you. He must have made the jump from the broken ladder.

'I've just seen Martha!' he says, excitedly. 'Akemi and Teah are waiting for us at the top! This way!' You scramble out of the carriage and follow Payton up the steep track — to the very top of the coaster!

Turn to 17.

5 Stepping out of the TARDIS, you are quite taken aback to discover that you are not where you were before. Apart from anything else, you seem to be inside a building... a very dark and dirty-looking hospital.

'This is like being back at work,' says Martha, her feet sticking to the filthy floor as she walks down the corridor. 'Only someone hasn't been doing their job!'

The truth is, it looks like no one's been doing anything in here for years. Least of all helping anyone get better.

You stop dead in your tracks.

'What is it?' Martha wants to know.

You point up ahead. You can see a man, dressed like a security guard — the kind who might park an armoured truck outside a bank. His eyes are covered by large, mirror-lensed goggles which make him look menacing — and he might be carrying some sort of weapon. He appears to be looking for something — but he hasn't spotted you yet.

If you want to follow him, turn to 85. If you'd rather try a nearby door, turn to 76.

6 You watch Cade make the jump first in the mantis. He takes a big run up and — boom! He bounces the vehicle off its back legs, right on the edge of the headland. The mantis flies through the air and lands on a platform — about halfway up the pipes. He made it, easily.

You follow his example, getting up as much speed as you can in your vehicle and then hitting the button to jump at the last possible moment. All those hours playing computer games at home were not wasted!

But it's too soon to congratulate yourself. You lose control of the locust in the air and miss the upper platform, crashing badly on a lower one. You hop out of your vehicle but, luckily, the grub is crawling up, slowly, between the pipes!

You hop into the cab with the Doctor, not a moment too late, as your vehicle explodes in a ball of flame. The grub creeps up the pipes through a portal to the Up Side…

Turn to 68.

7 You creep out of the store cupboard and close the door behind you. You follow the turn taken by the security guard, taking one last look around for the angry gang of hooded people. There's no sign of them — they must have skulked off in the opposite direction.

The corridor ends in a flight of stairs. The only way is up. You must be in the basement.

The Doctor leads the way up the stairs. You follow close behind, taking in the dirt-streaked walls, the grubby charts and litter-strewn floor. Martha follows on behind.

You head on up to the ground floor of the hospital. No light comes through the windows so it must be night-time. There's no sign of the security guard.

'Which way now?' asks Martha. You are standing underneath a cracked sign for Audiology, Radiology, Cardiology and... Car Parking.

You leave the creepy hospital and head towards the car park.

Turn to 43.

8 The Sun Temple stands in the middle of a vast desert. Dotted around are tall buildings that look as though they might be made of black glass. There are no roads connecting any of the buildings, but some silver bubbles are moving across the dazzlingly blue sky — you have no idea how far away they are, or how fast they're moving, because you don't know how big they are.

The place is deserted. Where is everyone?

'Nobody leaves their building complex,' says Akemi. 'Up here, everyone is afraid.'

You ask what they have to be afraid of.

'Other people,' says Akemi. 'That's all there really is to be scared about up here — we have created the perfect artificial environment. A beautiful second surface, up above the shoddy old one. Everything here is sterile, secure and safe. And it drives me crazy. That's why I started making illegal trips to the Down Side. Up here, everyone wants to be alone. But down there, people live together — as families, in colonies.'

'The darkness is changing people,' says the Doctor.

'It's true,' says Akemi. 'But it's not much better on the Up Side. Of course we are more comfortable, but our senses have been dulled. We eat well but we can no longer taste it... There are no young people, because hardly anyone can have children… and even fewer people actually want a family. They prefer to be alone.'

'That's sad,' says Martha, from the stairs of the Sun Temple. 'But what can be done about it?'

'That's where me and Teah come in,' says Akemi. 'I fell in love with her the moment we met. I'm hoping that my parents will respect our relationship. I am their only child and, when they see that we are married, perhaps that will set an example and change the attitudes of the Upsiders. You never know — maybe we can bring the two Sides back together!'

'Who are your parents?' says Martha. 'Are they important?'

Turn to 99 to find out.

9 You start climbing the rollercoaster, hoping Martha will follow your example.

After a couple of minutes, you're able to stop and sit on the track of the abandoned rollercoaster. Akemi is waiting for you, scanning the area down below through his goggles.

'The Downsiders won't follow us,' he says. 'They are weak from lack of light. Plus, they are afraid of what may come down, if they venture up here!'

You ask him what they might be afraid of.

'Drones,' says Akemi. 'Robot guards that protect the Up Side.'

Akemi sees the look on your face and says, 'Don't worry, I deactivated a whole bunch of them on my way down. We just have to get Teah and Payton to the Up Side, and then —'

You stop listening as you spot a shadowy figure. It seems to float towards you through the structure of the coaster.

To run away down the track, turn to 54.
To stay with Akemi, turn to 50.

10 You watch as the Doctor is swallowed up by the darkness ahead. It is gloomy outside but relatively light compared to being inside the ghost train. There must be a bit of light coming from somewhere.

You look up to the sky. There's no sign of any sun, moon or stars — just a steely greyness that makes you feel as though you're under a giant roof.

There's no wind and very little sound. You are aware of the noises you make as you move about: the rustling of your clothes and the crunch of crushed paper cups and broken glass under your feet.

You stop moving. But the rustling and crunching stops a moment later. You feel the hairs on the back of your neck stand up. There's someone behind you.

To spin around to see who is there, turn to 31. To hurry into the ghost train and find the Doctor, turn to 15.

11 You turn right. You can't see Martha anywhere. Everything is covered in mirrored panels — even the floor and ceiling. You almost feel as though you might be floating... but walking smack into a glass panel reminds you that the space around you is far from infinite.

Matching up what you can see (an illusion of space) with what you can feel (the solid walls of a narrow corridor) makes you feel dizzy... it doesn't help that you can see shadowy figures all around. But it's just your reflection... isn't it?

A pale, teenage girl in a flowing black dress appears in front of you, reaching out to you with a hand that trails long white strands of hair! You jump back from the strange figure... bump your head on the corner of a mirrored panel behind you... and black out.

Turn to 28.

12 You are amazed to discover that a different-looking world awaits you outside the TARDIS. You're not sure where you are but, somehow, you're not where you were before.

Wherever you are, it is dark. As your eyes begin to adjust, you see an arrangement of stones ahead of you... and then... a small chapel.

You're in a graveyard.

You gasp.

'What's up?' asks Martha. You want to say that you think you just saw a figure in dark robes slip out through the door of the chapel. But it was so quick, you're not sure if you really saw it all. So you don't say anything.

The Doctor strides ahead towards the chapel. You feel like hanging back but Martha grabs your arm and together you follow the Doctor through the old wooden door. It's even darker inside.

Turn to 90 to follow the Doctor. Turn to 33 to follow Martha.

13 Martha leads the way down from the choir stalls and you are only too glad to follow her.

Back in the graveyard you look up to the choir stalls. A flickering light appears behind the stained glass window. The Doctor must be up there, and it looks like he's found a candle.

As the light moves about you can see a picture in the remaining panels of glass. There are some large, menacing figures at the top of the window, and some pale, twisted figures, squashed into small spaces down below. Something about this mysterious scene makes you shudder.

The Doctor strides out of the chapel, his coat-tails flying out behind him. You and Martha both cry out, as you realise the figure in the choir stalls cannot be the Doctor.

'What?' says the Doctor. 'I thought you'd be happy to see me!'

You both point up to the window. The candle suddenly snuffs out and the shadowy figure disappears back into the blackness.

Turn to 2.

14 You turn left. A dull light hangs from the ceiling in the centre of a circular room. At least, it looks like a circular room — but you're not sure if this isn't just another trick being played by the mirrors...

You're standing alongside Martha. She grabs your arm and squeezes tightly, but you hardly even notice because you're both looking at the same thing...

A shadowy figure flitting about the space! The ghostly image seems to pass right through you.

Then, underneath the light, the shadowy apparition solidifies into the shape of a pale, teenage girl in a black flowing dress. Her eyes are unusually large with huge black pupils. She holds up a thin, trembling hand, trailing long strands of white hair.

You recoil from the strange girl and slip on the glass floor. You fall backwards and bump your head on the mirrored panel behind you... then black out.

Turn to 28.

15 You take a deep breath and follow the Doctor into the dark tunnel of the ghost train. You can't see anything at first, but then you make out a light from the Doctor's torch bobbing about just up ahead.

The Doctor is examining one of the ghost train's exhibits. Relieved to see him, you hurry towards the light. You stumble over the train tracks, struggling to keep your balance.

You manage to stay upright and walk more carefully towards the Doctor. You get a good look at what he is studying — a life-size figure in dark robes, just like the one you saw leaving the chapel earlier on.

Suddenly, the monk-like figure raises its arm in greeting!

You shriek and jump back. Your heel catches the track and you fall backwards into the blackness. There's a white flash behind your eyes as you bump your head on something solid.

Turn to 28.

You follow the Doctor and Payton around to the other side of the anti-gravity unit. You try to get a good look at it, but all you can see is a black, rubber-coated box — a bit like a car battery, only much bigger — near the base of a rickety old rollercoaster. You stop when you are quite some distance away from the Downsiders.

'Teah's colony is weak and cannot move fast,' whispers Payton. 'But their senses are highly developed.'

'That explains why her eyes are so large,' says the Doctor, 'and her hair—'

'It helps with her sense of touch,' says Payton, 'like a cat's whiskers.'

You ask about the strange clacking noise and Payton explains that it helps the Downsiders to find their way about in the dark. 'So we'd better get going,' says Payton.

'I'm not going anywhere without Martha,' says the Doctor.

To stay with the Doctor, turn to 53. To go with Payton, turn to 91.

You are reunited with your friends, old and new, at the highest point of the rollercoaster. Akemi is carrying Teah. He sets her down but she keeps an arm around him. She looks weak, exhausted.

Akemi has a quiet word with Payton, who comes over to you. He explains that Teah is upset. She knows her colony will not accept her relationship with Akemi but she still feels sad about leaving them behind.

And there's a problem with Akemi's escape route. The Drones — the robot guards that protect the Up Side — have recalled the Drone Wagon which Akemi hijacked to sneak down here.

'There's no way up from here without the Wagon,' Akemi says. 'It looks like this is the end of the line for us today.' He looks around nervously. 'The Drones could come back at any minute. If they catch us, we've had it.'

The Doctor frowns and surveys the view. You can tell he's thinking about something and he's not prepared to give up hope just yet. You try and see what he might be looking at...

You know you are high up, yet there isn't much of a view, just darkness above you and darkness below. It's a bit like being in the middle of the sea — you know you would sink if you stepped off the boat, yet the water looks as solid as the deck.

You try to explain this to Martha. She understands exactly.

'It almost makes you want to jump out into the darkness,' she says, 'doesn't it?'

'Good,' says the Doctor, 'because that's exactly what we're going to do.'

'You've got to be kidding,' laughs Martha.

If you threw a bottle cap at an anti-gravity unit earlier on, turn to 27. If you didn't, turn to 70.

18 The security guard says he means you no harm. He asks you if you are 'Upsiders'.

'What's an Upsider?' Martha wants to know. The security guard laughs. 'Seriously,' says Martha, 'explain to us as if we were from another planet or... time.' The Doctor gives Martha a hard stare. She shrugs.

The security guard explains, 'That black box you were just trying to get a look at? That's an anti-gravity unit — it's protected by a force field.'

You wonder why the unit needs protecting.

'Anti-gravity units are very important,' says the security guard. 'They keep up the Up Side!' You look blank, so he continues. 'When anti-gravity technology was invented, so was the Up Side. It was supposed to be the answer to our housing problems. But only a few people could afford to move up there. Those few people were greedy, and they kept on building — creating more and more space for themselves. And as the Up Side grew, so the people on the Down Side became sick.'

'No wonder,' says the Doctor, 'they are starved of natural light!'

'There are regular food drops,' says the guard. 'Drone ships bring down food parcels and the odd energy cell. Upsiders may be in better health but living apart from each other has taken its toll in other ways. Upsiders are dying out too.'

Martha has a question, 'So, who are you?'

'My name is Rafal — you can call me Raf,' he shakes your hand and you say your name. When the Doctor introduces himself, Raf becomes very excited. 'A doctor! Perfect! Then you might be able to help me on my mission, if you are willing.'

The Doctor looks at you and Martha. You both give a thumbs up, so you follow Raf away from the deserted car park. You allow yourself one last look around to the hospital and the anti-gravity unit... just in time to see several hooded figures disappear into the darkness.

Go to 97.

Cade pilots the mantis, Martha takes a dragonfly thing, and the Doctor gets inside something that looks like a grub. All of these vehicles are very ad hoc. The controls of your wasp-like vehicle are similar to an old games console that you used to play, so you get the hang of piloting it pretty quickly.

For the sake of fuel, you all agree not to try out the flying mechanisms of your vehicles for the time being. But still, they all move surprisingly quickly across land. You travel beyond the harbour until you can see the water fields — thick pipes, with maintenance platforms, that rise out of the stagnant sea up into the darkness above.

The water fields are about 500 metres off the coast. You talk with your companions, over your headset, about what to do next. You are given a choice — risk flying out to them in your untested wasp-like vehicle or squeeze in with the Doctor in the grub.

To risk flying, turn to 46. To join the Doctor, turn to 83.

20 You push open the door and step boldly into the room. You can see a window through which a person could climb... tanning beds... a few personal belongings...

Your thoughts are interrupted as someone flicks you with a towel. It really stings your arm! In the moment you are distracted, a woman elbows you in the ribs and barges past you through the door.

She has a child in her arms, and she is dressed in tatty black clothes. As she runs down the corridor, she reminds you of a big black bird taking flight. Raf tries to stop her but she ducks under his arms — and runs straight into Martha.

It must be Martha's medical training as she says something to the woman that calms her. Within a minute, Martha is holding the child and the woman — obviously tired from hiding out and relieved to be found by someone who might be able to help — is hugging Martha.

Turn to 47.

21 Outside the store cupboard, the corridor is now quiet and empty. You head after the angry mob. You follow some stairs up to the ground floor of the hospital — you must have been in the basement.

No light comes through the windows of the hospital. It must be night-time. You've lost sight of the group but — wait a minute! There's a straggler — an old woman with a bad limp.

'Hey!' says Martha. 'Wait!'

The old woman turns around, looking at you with huge, black eyes. She opens her mouth — revealing rotten, black teeth — and a pink tongue flicks out, as though she is tasting the air between you.

'You are no friend of ours,' she hisses, and you can smell her breath, even from a couple of metres away. 'You don't belong here.'

She hobbles away and seems to disappear into the shadows before you can give chase. It seems like a good idea to leave the hospital.

Turn to 43.

22 You set off down the twisting stone stairs of the lighthouse. It is hard, as so little light comes through the windows of the building. An arched doorway, about halfway down the structure, leads to some sort of living space.

The Doctor pulls a torch from his pocket and a circle of light opens out between the three of you. The Doctor swings the beam of light around the room.

It looks like the place has been abandoned in a hurry. There are a few neatly made beds and a couple of half-eaten meals. And the food hasn't gone off yet, so there must have been someone here not long ago.

'It's like the Marie Celeste in here,' says Martha.

You pick up a pair of unusual-looking binoculars and show them to the Doctor.

'These are sonic binoculars,' says the Doctor, examining them with his sonic screwdriver, 'and they're broken. Unfortunately, I can't fix them.' But he slips the binoculars into his coat pocket anyway and you exit the lighthouse.

Turn to 81.

23 You head over to the hooded man. The clothes he's wearing look like they've been made up out of a pile of other old garments. He flips back his hood. His eyes are unusually large and his skin is so pale you can see the blue veins underneath. His hair is long and silvery-white — although he doesn't seem very old. He asks you what you were doing in the hospital.

'I'm a doctor,' bluffs Martha.

The hooded man is very excited about this and he flicks out his tongue, spreading drool over his chin.

The security guard approaches. The hooded man suddenly turns angry and produces a weird-looking weapon. You've never seen anything like it before. It looks as homemade as his clothes.

The Doctor asks the man to calm down but he runs away, waving the weapon at all of you and urging you to 'stay away from the child'. What does he mean?

Turn to 18.

24 | The Doctor waves the sonic screwdriver around the edge of the force field.

'As I said, I've seen something like this before on Sepulgiarius... and it was an environmental disaster there too,' says the Doctor. 'This is an A.G.U. — an anti-gravity unit. It's probably one of many, holding something up. Not the road, something above that — something so big it's blocking out the sky.' The Doctor stops as the sonic screwdriver unlocks an invisible maintenance 'doorway' in the force field. You follow him to get a closer look.

The Doctor cries out, 'It's been sabotaged!' A small spider-like device is attached to the A.G.U. The Doctor deactivates the device with his sonic screwdriver and holds it up. 'We arrived here just in time. This was about to block the anti-gravity field... and who knows what might have come crashing down!'

You walk back towards Martha. Your relief at averting a potential disaster is brief, as a large, shadowy figure steps out of the shadows...

Turn to 60.

Akemi takes one of Teah's arms, and you take the other. You help her up the steps of a vast sandstone building with a huge dome. Inside it's cool and Teah sits down, gratefully.

'Thank you,' she says. 'I don't know where you three are from, but it's been great having you around.'

You leave Martha chatting with the others and wander around the Temple. Your footsteps echo in the vast space. The floors and the walls of the Temple are immaculately tiled and everything is clean and bright. You wonder who keeps the place like this — because there doesn't seem to be anyone else around.

Sunlight streams through vast panels of stained glass depicting scenes of what look like kings and queens — each one alone in a tall tower or on a plinth.

Martha calls you over. It's time to go. Payton is looking after Teah. So you say goodbye to Teah and Payton and follow Martha and Akemi back outside.

Turn to 8.

Payton has discovered an emergency exit ladder. It runs up the inside of the rollercoaster. The Doctor is the first to start climbing. You go second. Payton follows on behind.

With all three of you on the ladder, you can hear the rusty metal and wood of the old rollercoaster groaning.

As the Doctor climbs ahead, a rung of the ladder comes away from under his foot. You manage to dodge it as it falls, but it hits Payton on the shoulder, almost knocking him off balance.

When you come to the part of the ladder where the rung is missing, you have to take a big step up. You concentrate on the ladder above, where it disappears into the darkness. You dare not look down.

The Doctor sees that you have stopped climbing and he asks if you are alright.

To nod, yes, turn to 61. To shake your head, no, turn to 40.

27 | You mention picking up a bottle cap earlier on. You describe how you threw the cap against the force field around the A.G.U. and how it just, sort of... bounced off.

'And so?' says the Doctor. You say that it made you wonder if... maybe... a person could do that.

'Exactly!' says the Doctor clapping you on the back. 'I knew you were bright! We're going to slip into the anti-gravity stream and bounce — all the way to the Up Side! Right, kids?'

'Well,' says Akemi, nervously, 'I've never done it before but we could give it a go!'

'Do we have a choice?' asks Martha.

Akemi explains that you could wait for the next food drop from the Up Side, but you'd be running the risk of dealing with a fresh wave of Drones.

Are you prepared to make the leap of faith? Turn to 39. Or would you rather wait for the food drop? Turn to 86.

28 | **Y**our first waking thought is, 'Ow!'

You are lying on the ground between the ghost train and the hall of mirrors — and the back of your head hurts. Martha looks into your eyes and asks you some questions. You answer them easily.

She helps you up and you walk around a bit, and then she asks you the same questions again — checking you out for concussion. She explains that you fell and bumped your head. You were lucky not to have really hurt yourself!

Reassured you're OK, Martha leads you over to where the Doctor is talking with three strangers. With the Doctor are: a pale teenage girl dressed in black; a mysterious robed figure; and a man wearing white.

To go to the young woman, turn to 71. If you want to approach the man wearing robes, turn to 3. If you'd rather approach the man dressed in white, turn to 88.

There's a loud whooshing noise. Your stomach lurches. The floor drops away from beneath your feet, then it suddenly rushes back up again, knocking you off balance. Martha puts an arm around you and holds you steady. The noise fades down to a gentle hum and the clanking and clicking of cooling machinery.

'Where are we?' asks Martha.

'I'm not sure,' says the Doctor, looking at you. 'Which button did you press?' You point to the red one. There's a pause and you wait to see if he's going to tell you off... but he just claps his hands and then rubs them together.

'Right!' he says, brightly. 'Well, before we can get you back to where we came from, we need to find out exactly where we are now.'

'Brilliant!' says Martha, her eyes sparkling as she holds open the TARDIS door. 'After you!' she says, and waves you through.

Turn to 12.

'Quick!' says Akemi, glancing over at the Downsiders gathering at the entrance to the funfair. 'If they catch me, I'm for it!'

'And what will they do to us?' wonders Martha.

Akemi doesn't reply. He's pulling his mirror-lensed goggles over his strange, milky eyes and leading Martha away. You take a quick look at the Downsiders. They look like Teah — with ghostly pale skin and dark, hollow eyes. You guess the light on the Up Side and the dark on the Down Side has been doing strange things to people's eyesight!

They move forward as a group. They flick out their tongues, tasting the air, and sweep the ground with the long hair that trails from their hands and some of their faces. Suddenly, the leader stops dead in his tracks — right where you were standing just a moment ago. It is as though he knows you were there — as though he has smelt you! He starts up with that strange clacking sound... and the Downsiders begin to run in your direction!

Race to catch up to Martha. Turn to 35.

31 You turn and see someone dressed from head to toe in white. Clean white boots, boiler suit, gloves and a backpack that wraps securely around his body. A white balaclava covers his head. The figure is moving stealthily towards the hall of mirrors... Martha is in there! You need to find her, before the mysterious stranger does!

You take a step forward but some old rubbish crunches beneath your feet. It only makes a small sound but the figure stops dead in his tracks, straightens up and turns to look right at you through mirror-lensed goggles.

You run into the ghost train, shouting for the Doctor. You race forward with your arms outstretched. You don't have time for your eyes to adjust to the darkness. You trip over the tracks of the ghost train. You fall into the blackness... there's a white flash behind your eyes as you bump your head on something hard.

Turn to 28.

32 You pass an eerily empty ticket booth. It feels strange to enter the ghost train with no one else around — it's a bit like being in a school or office after everyone's gone home.

The old turnstile rasps and scrapes as you push your way through. The train carriages are rusted on to their tracks and full of rubbish. The doors into the tunnel are hanging off their hinges.

As the Doctor pushes open one of the doors, it drops to the ground with a crash. He kicks it to one side and follows the tracks into the darkness. It's not too late to change your mind and turn back.

If you want to hang around outside the ghost train and see what happens, turn to 10. If you want to stick with the Doctor, turn to 15 before he gets away. If you'd rather leave the ghost train and check out the hall of mirrors with Martha, turn to 89.

33 'Hey,' says Martha, grabbing your wrist. 'I wonder what's up here?'

You follow close behind Martha as she runs up a flight of wooden stairs and discover that the stairs lead to the choir stalls and a large, detailed stained glass window. You notice the stained glass is in a state of disrepair. Some of the panels are missing, yet no breeze blows in from the outside.

You say that you bet the windows look great in the day, when the sun is shining through them.

'Yes!' says Martha. 'Or the moon.'

But there doesn't seem to be any moon in the sky outside. Or stars. Just... blackness.

'We'd be able to see these windows a lot better if there was a bit more light,' says Martha. 'Maybe we can find some candles.'

To follow Martha back downstairs, turn to 13. To hang back in the choir stalls, turn to 52.

34 You shuffle along behind Martha. She keeps her left hand against the mirrored wall. You do the same and the mirror feels cold and industrial — it makes the stone walls of the chapel seem almost homely in comparison.

In the dim light, it looks as though you are moving among an army of shadows — but it's only the reflections of the pair of you, bouncing between the mirrors.

Martha presses on, always looking ahead. But you can't help stopping and glancing over your shoulder. When you turn back, Martha has disappeared. All you can see is your own reflection looking back at you...

Where is Martha? You can't see her, but you hear her gasp. You can turn to the left or to the right. But which way did Martha go?

To go left, turn to 14. If you'd rather head right, turn to 11.

You can't see Martha anywhere. Confused — you stop walking and look left and right.

Suddenly, somebody grabs you and drags you under the scaffolding-like structure of the rollercoaster. It's Akemi and Martha. You fall over into a pile of stinking rubbish that has built up under the coaster.

'They can't see us here,' says Akemi, peering out into the gloom through his goggles and adjusting them with a dial on the side. 'Downsiders have a very strong sense of smell — this will cover our scent.'

Akemi starts rubbing rubbish all over himself. He urges you to do the same. He picks up sweet wrappers and lolly sticks, popcorn boxes and chip cones and presses them into your hands. This is crazy! You burst out laughing — you can't help it!

Akemi shushes you and whispers, 'Downsiders have also got excellent hearing!'

You cover your face and pull yourself together, trying to forget that you ever saw Martha rubbing a crisp packet against her hair.

'We have to get out of here,' says Akemi in hushed tones, 'and I know a way. Follow me!' Akemi begins to climb the rollercoaster structure, quickly and confidently, as though he might have done it a hundred times before.

Akemi is already well above the ground. As you look up, you realise you can't even see the top of the rollercoaster — it just disappears up into the darkness. Akemi stops and looks down. He beckons you to follow.

'I'm not climbing up there,' whispers Martha. 'No way!'

You wonder why not.

'It doesn't look safe,' explains Martha, looking around. 'There must be a better way — maybe a fire escape or something.'

The Downsiders are closing in on you... You'd better move. Quick!

To follow Akemi up the rollercoaster, turn to 9. To go with Martha, turn to 87.

When you're about twenty-five metres from the box, a strange thing happens. All three of you stop walking and fall backwards. It's as though there's an invisible mattress in the air and you just bounced off it!

You and Martha are both winded and burst out laughing in shock and surprise. Naturally you look to the Doctor for an explanation.

'A force field,' he says, 'protecting the unit.' He nods towards the black box.

'Perhaps that security building is guarding it as well,' says Martha.

'Could be,' says the Doctor, waving his sonic screwdriver about.

You suddenly realise that you are being watched. The security guard from the hospital is standing outside the nearby building. Another man, his face obscured by a black hood, is coming over the bank...

Both men shout out to you, 'Hey! Over here!'

Who do you go to? The hooded man? Turn to 23. Or the security guard? Turn to 18.

37 You try to head off the hooded Downsider, but he sidesteps you and races straight up to Althea. She hugs him, calling out his name, 'Andreas!'

The Drones have spotted you! Raf deactivates the first Drone the way he showed you — with a sharp kick to the back of the right knee joint. But you're too far away to deactivate the second Drone, as planned. The second Drone attempts to escape in the Wagon. The Doctor switches on the sunlamp. For a moment it looks like it's not going to work, but then the amplified UV rays block the Wagon's navigational system and it comes crashing down!

Martha hands Cal over to Andreas and covers for you. She deactivates the second Drone and throws it out of the cab. The Doctor and Raf jump into the Wagon. Martha, Althea, Andreas and Cal jump into the back, and the shell begins to come down… you roll under the gap of the shiny black shell just as it hisses back into place. Whoosh! The Doctor pilots the Wagon… to the Up Side!

Turn to 98.

You can't describe it exactly, but you have a strange feeling about the box. You feel as though something is stopping you from approaching it — even though you can't see any barriers.

The Doctor takes the broken sonic binoculars out of his pocket and hurls them at the box. You watch, agog, as they stop in mid-air and bounce off something... then come flying back in your direction! You duck, and feel the binoculars riffle your hair as they fly over your head... and smash to bits on the ground behind you.

'Ah, well,' the Doctor shrugs. 'I knew they'd be useful for something! In this case — demonstrating the force field surrounding that box!'

The Doctor begins walking around the edge of the force field in an anticlockwise direction.

To accompany the Doctor, turn to 63. To walk around the force field in a clockwise direction, turn to 41.

'OK,' says Akemi. 'This is it.'

'I'm coming with you,' says Teah. 'Whatever happens — I want us to be together.'

Teah and Akemi hug the Doctor and then Martha and you. They take a small bow before Payton. Akemi and Teah hold hands, step off the edge of the rollercoaster, and fall… upwards!

You stare, open-mouthed, up into the blackness that has just swallowed them. It looks like the Doctor's idea has worked! Payton congratulates the Doctor, before following Akemi's lead. His black robes spread out in the air, making him look like a giant bird as he zips upwards.

How could you not want to do that? Martha looks at you, with a big grin right across her face. You used to think rollercoasters were exciting! This is something else! Martha jumps into the void. You can hear her laughing as she goes — loving every second of it!

It's your turn. You look at the Doctor. He smiles and nods. You take a deep breath. And you jump.

Turn to 49.

40 You shake your head. Your feet feel frozen to a rung of the ladder. You dare not look up or down. You just stare straight ahead into the structure of the rollercoaster.

A face with hollow black eyes floats up in front of you. You press yourself up against the ladder, hoping the ghostly figure will pass by. But it doesn't... it reaches out and touches you with a shimmering white hand...

It's only Teah! Her black clothes, pale face and silvery hair gave you a scare! You almost forget to hold the ladder as the fear drains out of you. But the Doctor is there now to hold you and stop you from falling.

What a relief! Teah shows you a twisting maintenance path inside the structure. She tells you that it leads to the highest point of the rollercoaster and that you will be safer there. The three of you follow her, all the way up.

Turn to 17.

41 The Doctor walks around the mysterious black box. You and Martha set off in the opposite direction.

'This is an anti-gravity unit,' the Doctor shouts across to you, 'or an A.G.U. It's protected by a force field because it's holding up something big — The Doctor stops dead and speaks urgently. 'We have to get up close to the A.G.U.!'

You ask what's wrong and the Doctor says, 'There's something unusual stuck to the A.G.U.! I think it might have been sabotaged!' Martha picks up a stick from the ground and begins running round the edge of the force field — a bit like a kid trailing a stick against a fence.

'Here!' shouts Martha. The Doctor hurries over and uses the sonic screwdriver to unlock an invisible maintenance 'door' in the force field. He races to the A.G.U. and yanks away a small spider-like device. You ask Martha how she knew what to do.

'I just guessed,' she shrugs. You are about to tell her how smart she is when you notice you are no longer alone...

Turn to 60.

Stepping out of the TARDIS, you are surprised to discover that you are not where you were before. It doesn't even seem to be the same time of day... it's very dark.

It takes you a moment to realise that you are inside a building — because you are surrounded by glass. It's the giant-sized lamp that makes you realise you're in the top of a lighthouse!

'Wow!' says the Doctor. 'Good going, new kid! It's a long time since I visited a lighthouse! So long ago, it's just a... foggy memory!'

The Doctor chuckles to himself. Martha rolls her eyes at you. 'Well, we're definitely on Earth,' says the Doctor. 'But I'm not sure when.'

The view from the top of the lighthouse is not as pleasant as you might have expected. There's no moon. No stars. And you can't hear the tide. Everything is dark and still.

To look around the top of the lighthouse, turn to 59. To explore further down, go to 22.

'**W**here are we anyway?' says Martha, as you exit the hospital into a deserted car park. 'And when?'

The Doctor tells you that you are definitely on Earth. And, you observe, wherever you are it is dark. There doesn't seem to be any moon in the sky outside. Or stars. Just... blackness. You wonder if maybe there's an eclipse.

'Something like that,' says the Doctor, looking up at the starless sky.

There's no breeze, no noise. Just the shells of dumped cars, with anything that might be of value looted from them long ago. It's like an abandoned set for a film about the end of the world.

Over on a bank of dead, yellow grass is a black, rubber-coated box — a bit like a car battery, only much bigger — with one blinking green light on it. On the other side of the car park is a building with a sign saying 'SECURIT'. You suppose the 'Y' has been snapped off.

To check out the box, turn to 36. To investigate the security building, turn to 93.

44 | Martha takes up the oars and pushes the boat out of the cove in the lighthouse rocks. You can see that she is struggling with the oars, even though there is no tide. You ask her if she is OK and suddenly, one of the oars slips into the sea and sinks below the surface — even though it should have floated away.

'That was weird,' says Martha. 'Something pulled the oar out of my hand...' With a stomach-churning slurp, something in the water suddenly sucks the second oar out of Martha's hand... leaving you stranded. You all look over the edge of the boat and see some tentacles slip along the side of the boat.

The Doctor explains that deep sea creatures seem to have been drawn to the surface by the darkness. He uses the sonic screwdriver to power up the motor and get you to the shore... The stench there is worse than anywhere. Since there is no wind, or tide, there is a build-up of dark yellow scum at the edge of the sea. You are only too glad to climb out of the boat and drag it up the litter-strewn beach.

Turn to 96.

45 Now you've been to the Up Side, you realise how grim it is down below. You hadn't noticed quite how bad the Down Side smelt when you were here before. You must have become used to it. It's amazing how quickly a person can adapt to their surroundings.

You climb out of the rollercoaster carriage, glad that the Doctor was able to loosen the wheels with his sonic screwdriver, saving you the climb down.

'Back to the TARDIS, then?' says Martha.

'Yes,' says the Doctor, ruffling your hair. 'I think we'd better take this one home.'

As you walk together through the dark you suddenly remember that, when you first met the Doctor, you were running away from something. What was it?

'Oh, yes,' says the Doctor, stopping in his tracks, 'I forgot about that.' He frowns. Then smiles and sets off walking again. 'Come on, then! We'd better go and find out…!'

THE END... FOR NOW!

46 You watch Cade make the jump to the water fields, as the Doctor steers the grub vehicle into the sea. You and Martha allow yourselves a good long distance to get up some speed and then shoot your vehicles off the edge of the headland.

Your wasp vehicle roars and whines — but you're flying! And so is Martha... or she seems to be, but then she suddenly drops away beneath you!

You could easily make it to the upper platform on the water pipes but, once you've landed, you could never take off again. And so you turn your vehicle around in the air and look for Martha.

You can see now that she has crash-landed on a lower platform. Her vehicle is wrecked, but she is OK — and the Doctor is nearby with the grub. You steer the wasp around again and land perfectly and safely on the upper platform — then travel upwards through a portal to the other side...

Turn to 68.

Martha is carrying the child. He's about a year old and wrapped up in the Doctor's suit jacket. He is quiet and subdued, but perfectly healthy-looking. She tells you his name is Cal. Martha has given the woman her leather jacket. Her eyes are huge, with large black pupils. Her hair is silvery white and her skin is so thin you can see veins pulsing underneath.

You apologise to the woman for giving her a fright and tell her your name. She says her name is Althea. You can't help but notice that her tongue flicks out when she speaks.

'We have to get up to the drop point,' says Raf. 'If we hurry, we might just make the next food drop. We could sneak into the back of a Drone Wagon, or try to take control of one directly.'

'Right!' says the Doctor, and he turns to you. 'What do you think?'

To reach the Up Side by sneaking on to a Wagon, turn to 58. To try and commandeer a Wagon, turn to 67.

Cade's workshop is an abandoned warehouse in the dock. As he shows you around, he explains the reasoning behind his work.

'Insects are the only things to thrive in this environment, so I have devised these vehicles in an attempt to help Downsiders survive. Materials and fuel have become scarce — most colonies don't even have proper clothes to wear, let alone transport like this,' he taps the shell of a creepy-looking contraption — and something drops off the side of it, landing on the floor with a clang. Cade clears his throat and says, 'Yes, well… some of these vehicles need proper testing.'

Martha wants to know what the Doctor has in mind. 'To take these vehicles to the Up Side and then…' he trails off. 'Well, first things first! Is there any way to reach the Up Side?'

'No,' says Cade. 'Why else would I have been trying to deactivate the A.G.U. and bring a section of the Up Side down?'

'There must be something that links both sides,' says the Doctor. 'A facility that services some basic human need.'

'Water?' says Martha.

'Bingo!' says the Doctor. 'You must share water with the Up Side?'

'Yes,' says Cade. 'The Up Side sends down its waste via the water fields — and draws up sea water for cooling. But the fields are out to sea and I don't have enough energy to reach them. All my vehicles are hybrid — but my energy cells are dead and I'm almost out of liquid fuel.'

'We'll see about that!' says the Doctor, rolling up his sleeves. 'Show me what you've got!'

While the Doctor and Cade talk animatedly about 'bioethanol to petroleum ratios', you and Martha look around the workshop. All the vehicles are made up of bits of old cars and other obsolete junk. You have to choose a vehicle to take to the water fields.

To take a locust-like vehicle, turn to 94.
To pilot a wasp-like vehicle, turn to 19.

| **W**umph!

It's a bit like rolling out of bed asleep and finding yourself dazed on the bedroom floor — only you're a long, long way from home…

You slip off the cushion of the anti-gravity field and land on the Up Side with a bump. This is the new surface. A world above the world. It is clean and sparse and blindingly bright.

You shield your eyes from the sun. The air is warm. You breathe like you've never breathed before. It's like you've been born again. No wonder Akemi wanted Teah to come here.

You look around. Everyone's made it — you, the Doctor, Martha, Akemi, Teah and Payton.

'Quick,' says Payton. 'Let's get Teah inside the Sun Temple. The light is too much for her.'

'Imagine,' says the Doctor. 'She's never seen the sun before.'

To help Teah into the Sun Temple, turn to 25. To stay with the Doctor, turn to 8.

The shadowy figure is Teah, approaching you via some sort of maintenance walkway. She is weak from the climb and upset about running away from her colony. She is relieved to see you both. Akemi jumps up and embraces her.

'We must keep going to the highest point of the rollercoaster,' explains Akemi. He says that he will help Teah, and that you must follow him closely. 'Tread only where I have trodden before,' he says. 'And hold on to the same struts — parts of the structure are rotten and may not hold your weight.'

Even carrying Teah, Akemi makes climbing the rollercoaster look easy. You find it hard — but at least concentrating on Akemi's movements, making sure you copy them exactly, stops you from thinking about the drop below!

As you climb higher and higher, you hear the clacking and hissing of Teah's Downsider colony fade away far beneath...

Turn to 17.

51 You press the yellow button and nothing happens. The Doctor and Martha look at each other and then look at you. The Doctor opens his mouth to say something, when the air around you explodes with the noise of machinery and your stomach lurches like it does when you go over a big drop on a rollercoaster.

Then, just as suddenly as it began, the noise stops and the whole room goes still and quiet again. You feel dizzy. Martha holds your shoulders and steadies you.

'It feels weird, doesn't it?' she says, smiling. 'I'll never forget my first journey in time!'

You laugh. What is she talking about, 'journey in time'?

'Now,' says the Doctor, turning to you, 'if you'd care to step outside for a minute, maybe we can find out where you've taken us!'

The Doctor holds open the door of the TARDIS and you step out into the unknown.

Turn to 42.

52 You listen as Martha clumps back down the wooden stairs. You take a closer look at the few panels of the stained glass window that remain fixed in their lead frames. You can make out some happy-looking, angelic figures, floating by on clouds. Lower down are some sad and angry people. Maybe the window is just dirty, but the people below look as though they are being swallowed up by shadows.

You peer through an empty panel to the graveyard. You can just make out a figure down below. It must be Martha, so you call her name.

She replies, 'Hey!' She's right behind you. She must have crept back upstairs. You almost jump out of your skin.

Martha's holding a candle but says she couldn't find anything to light it with. You say you thought you saw her outside and you point through the window... but there's no one out there.

'Come on,' says Martha. 'We'd better find the Doctor.'

Turn to 2.

53 | As the Doctor looks around for Martha, you ask him why he doesn't seem worried by the approaching Downsiders.

'They're looking for us using that clacking sound,' says the Doctor. 'They listen for the sound bouncing back. I can send them off-beam using this — ' The Doctor waves his sonic screwdriver and grins. He points it in the direction of the ghost train and you notice the Downsiders tilting their heads and then shuffling off in that direction.

You pick up an old bottle cap and toss it at the anti-gravity unit. You are amazed to see how it bounces off the force field, seemingly in mid-air. You wonder what it might be like if a person threw themselves into the anti-gravity field? Would they bounce off?

Payton waves at you from the helter-skelter. 'I think I know where Martha's gone!' he whispers. 'She's with Akemi and Teah... up there!' Payton points towards the top of the old rollercoaster.

Turn to 26.

You jump up, and run away from the spooky figure. Slipping and sliding down the rollercoaster track, you hear someone call your name. It's Martha. She's climbing a maintenance ladder that runs up through the centre of the structure.

Below her on the ladder are the Doctor and Payton. You explain that you were running away from a dark figure — maybe a Downsider or... what was it Akemi said? A Drone!

Payton asks, 'Are you sure it wasn't Teah?'

You flush. It might have been Teah. You ran away before you could find out.

'She's good at making spooky appearances,' says Martha.

'Come on,' says Payton. 'We must join them at the top of the coaster.'

The four of you climb the maintenance ladder. It's rusted and rickety and you can see why Akemi decided to climb the structure instead. But all of you make it to the highest point of the rollercoaster.

Turn to 17.

55 | All three of you get into the lift. It's a big hospital lift — big enough to carry a patient on a wheeled bed.

The button marked 'B' is illuminated — so you guess you're in the basement. Martha presses the button for the ground floor. Nothing happens. The security guard is closing in on you… maybe he won't be so scary. You start to think of things to say to him, to explain why you're there. But there's no need.

The Doctor punches the 'close' button and the lift doors slide shut with a 'whumph!'

The lift wheezes into life and you hear the scurrying of animals — or large insects — being disturbed in the lift shaft above you.

The lift carries you up to the ground floor with the kind of grinding and screeching that suggests it hasn't been used for a long time.

You are relieved to get out of the lift and leave the hospital through the nearest door.

Turn to 43.

56 The Doctor follows you around the back of the tanning salon. Just like everywhere you have been, the back of the shop is depressingly full of rubbish and debris.

There is a window, but it is quite high up. You have to climb on to the Doctor's shoulders to look into it.

Through the grimy window you can just about see a back room, with a couple of sun beds and... nothing else. You are about to climb down again when something stops you...

You think you might have heard something... did you?

Yes! There it is again! It sounds like a... child, coughing.

And now you look again, the window is closed but it's been opened recently. You can see footprints in the dust on the window sill.

Do you tap on the window? Turn to 79. Or would you rather return to the front of the salon? Turn to 62.

| You and Martha move forward to examine the box…

'Wait!' shouts the Doctor. And a very strange thing happens… both you and Martha stop in mid-stride and… bounce! It is as though you just ran smack into the wall of an invisible bouncy castle!

You both fall backwards and land on your bottoms. Now you wish you really were wearing your skateboarding gear! You stand up and brush yourself down, then give Martha a hand up.

'Sorry for laughing,' the Doctor chuckles, 'but I did try to warn you! I've seen something like this before. There's a force field protecting this device. But I think I might be able to find a way through.'

Do you want to go with the Doctor to find a way through the force field and check out the box? Turn to 24. Or would you rather wait with Martha? Turn to 78.

Raf tells you, 'The Drone Wagons are piloted by robot Drones. They drop supplies to the Downsiders once a week. To avoid trouble, it's always in a different location. I know the next drop is going to be here.' Raf taps his nose. 'Insider info.'

This is all good to know. But it doesn't prepare you for the appearance of the Drone Wagon! Able to 'fly' using anti-gravity technology, it is completely silent. And it looks like a giant cockroach!

The Wagon touches down and opens up. A Drone — a silvery humanoid robot — unloads boxes of supplies.

On a signal from Raf, you run into the back of the Wagon. He leads the way. You help Althea. Martha carries Cal. The Doctor comes last... but he isn't alone. An angry-looking Downsider rolls under the gap of the Wagon's shell just as it snaps into place — his appearance could disrupt your mission! Raf dives towards the Downsider...

To stop him, go to 95. If you don't want to stop him, turn to 64.

Martha picks up a small pair of binoculars. She takes a look through them, but can't see anything.

'Sonic binoculars,' says the Doctor, examining them with his sonic screwdriver. 'I'm afraid they're broken beyond repair.' He slips them into his coat pocket anyway.

Looking around the top of the lighthouse, you discover that the bulb has long since been spent. It is burnt out. Dead.

You discuss the redundant light bulb as you walk down the spiral staircase that wraps itself around the core of the lighthouse.

'In itself, it is not too worrying,' says the Doctor. 'After all, even in your day, most lighthouses had become automated. This one is clearly defunct. Maybe it's just someone's home now.'

You remind the Doctor of satellite navigation. Maybe ships stopped needing lighthouses altogether.

'Or maybe they just stopped making light bulbs,' jokes Martha. 'You know, to save the environment.'

However, as you exit the lighthouse, you discover that, wherever you are right now, the environment seems to have become the last thing on anyone's mind...

Turn to 81.

60 A three-metre-high, insect-like machine looms over Martha!

The mechanical mantis takes a swipe at you with one of its formidable front legs. But the Doctor dives in with the sonic screwdriver. The mechanical insect judders to a halt as its belly snaps open with a hiss.

The pilot of the mantis-vehicle-thing is pale and weak-looking. Although he appears to be human, he doesn't look like anyone you've ever seen before. His eyes are unusually large with big, black pupils.

The Doctor waves the device he just removed from the A.G.U. 'Are you behind this?' he demands to know. The pale man nods and you notice his chin is covered in saliva. The Doctor shouts, 'If this thing had blocked out the anti-gravity field, whatever is up there would have come crashing down to kill us all!'

'That's right,' says the man. His tongue flicks out of his mouth when he speaks, as though he is tasting the air. 'But I might have seen the sky for a moment, before I died.'

The Doctor deflates a little. 'I understand why you are angry,' he says, calmly, 'but are there not people up there?'

'Yes, but what do they care about us?' says the man. 'We're dying down here!'

As the Doctor and the stranger talk about the situation, you begin to understand what's going on. There are anti-gravity units everywhere, keeping what is known as the Up Side in place. A few, well-off humans live on the vast surface of the Up Side, while colonies of pale 'Downsiders' scrabble to exist in the darkness below.

The man — whose name is Cade — has lost all his friends, his whole colony. 'And I'm so weak,' he says, slapping the side of the mantis, 'I need this thing just to get around!'

'Have you any more of those?' says the Doctor.

'Oh, yes!' says Cade. 'I never stop inventing things! I have been working on all kinds of prototypes!'

'Excellent,' says the Doctor. 'Show me!'

Turn to 48 to see Cade's workshop.

61 | You keep climbing.

Another rusty rung snaps out from under the Doctor's feet and whistles past your ear.

This time, as you swing your foot up at the part of the ladder where the rung broke off, you can feel the whole of the metal ladder pull away from the wooden structure.

There's a juddering snap — then the blood-curdling screech of twisting metal. A section of the ladder breaks away just above you and bends just below... leaving you holding on — and your feet swinging out into space.

You dare to look down. Directly below you is a section of rollercoaster track. It's not too big a drop.

'Hold on!' shouts the Doctor, hurrying further up the ladder.

Do you let go of the ladder and hope you'll land squarely on the track below? Turn to 92. Or would you rather 'hold on'? Turn to 4.

'This place has been unused for years,' says Raf, in front of the salon. 'But if the child's mother has got hold of an energy cell, she might have been able to get one of the sun lamps going.'

While Raf struggles to lift up the shutter at the front of the salon, Martha wanders around the back. The Doctor gently pushes Raf to one side and uses the sonic screwdriver to unlock the shutter and open the front door.

He holds the door open and you enter the reception. Everything is covered in a thick layer of dust. It's obvious that no one's been in the salon recently... at least, not through the front door...

Beyond the reception are several doors. You put your ear to each of them, one at a time. At the final door, you hear the sound of a child coughing.

To open the door, turn to 20. To knock first, turn to 82.

63 You walk with the Doctor in an anticlockwise direction around the mysterious black box. The Doctor waves his sonic screwdriver about, detecting the edge of the force field.

'This is an anti-gravity unit,' the Doctor explains, 'or an A.G.U. It must be one of many — holding something up. Not the road, something above that — something so big it's blocking out the sky.' The Doctor stops as the sonic screwdriver unlocks an invisible maintenance 'doorway' in the force field.

'Ah-ha! Now to take a closer look at the...' The Doctor stops talking and races across to the A.G.U. He starts working at it, frantically, with his sonic screwdriver. He yanks a small spider-like device away from the unit.

'That was too close for comfort,' shouts the Doctor. Before you can ask him what he has found, you suddenly realise that the three of you are being watched...

Turn to 60.

Raf uses a small device, strapped to the palm of his hand, to stun the Downsider.

'Hey!' says the Doctor, annoyed. 'That wasn't part of the plan!'

'Well, he wasn't part of the plan, either,' says Raf, rolling the Downsider over so you can see his face. Like Althea, he has pale skin and large eyes.

Althea gasps. 'It's Andreas — Cal's father!'

'Oops. Sorry!' says Raf. 'Don't worry, he's not hurt — just unconscious.'

'We were split up a few days ago, when we were on the run. You're not the first Upsider to come looking for us,' says Althea. 'We could see that Cal was something special, and he might be important to someone else — besides us. Andreas was adamant that Cal shouldn't be taken to the Up Side. "Why can't they come down here?" he said. And, of course, I couldn't stand for him to be taken from me.'

You feel the Drone Wagon touching down. It's time to find out how life is on the other Side…

Turn to 98.

A pre-programmed, pilotless Wagon carries you silently back to the place where you started your journey.

Althea, Andreas and Raf were all grateful to you for your kindness and bravery. But you're still not sure why little Cal is so important.

The Doctor explains to you, 'He is the last of a lineage descended from the President of the Up Side and a Downsider Rebel. The child contains the best of both sides.'

'I get it,' says Martha. 'His genes contain the pattern for what we recognise as "normal" — so that the human race can continue.'

'Rather than evolving into two separate races of Upsiders and Downsiders, that will both sicken and die out,' finishes the Doctor.

'Wow! It makes you think, doesn't it?' Martha says. 'I guess it wasn't a waste of time when I had to read all those papers on gene therapy!'

But there's still one thing you don't understand. If Cal is valuable to the Upsiders, how come they didn't make his passage to the Up Side any easier?

'Most of them don't want to believe that their possible future depends on a child they would have happily allowed to perish down here,' says the Doctor. 'The people who employed

Raf are a progressive party of Upsiders, who want to see both Sides united.'

You think about all of this as you leave the Wagon in the deserted car park and walk through the dirty hospital. It doesn't seem so creepy now, after all that you have seen. But the darkness and the shadows dredge up a distant memory...

When you first saw the Doctor he told you to run... wasn't there some sort of big shape, coming across the sky...?

'Oh, yes!' says the Doctor, stopping in his tracks, 'I'd forgotten about that! How exciting!'

The Doctor asks you if you're ready for another adventure and you grin and nod your head. He ruffles your hair and says, 'Great! I think you're going to be up to the challenge because, well, you've already helped save humankind once today!'

THE END

You take up the oars of the boat and sit with your back to the shore. The Doctor and Martha sit in the back of the boat, facing forward. Rowing is much harder work than you expected. As you dip the oars into the sea you can't help but notice that the surface is covered in a thick, jelly-like substance.

You begin to wonder — if this boat was shored up at the lighthouse — doesn't that mean that there was someone else there, apart from you? You look back at the lighthouse and, for a second, you're sure you see a dark, shrouded figure with a deathly pale face, in the top of the lighthouse... but before you can say anything to your companions, the figure disappears...

There is a build-up of dark yellow scum at the edge of the stagnant sea. You are only too glad when you reach the shore and drag the boat a way up the litter-strewn beach.

Turn to 96.

Raf has briefed you all well. Each Drone Wagon is piloted by two Drones. They are humanoid in appearance but, as they are robots, they can be deactivated.

You and Raf are going to deactivate the Drones, while Martha has the all important job of making sure Althea and Cal get on-board the Wagon unharmed. That's the plan.

Meanwhile, the Doctor is modifying a sunlamp with the sonic screwdriver. He hopes the amplified UV rays might interfere with the Wagon's navigational system, forcing the Wagon to make an emergency landing if it takes off without you.

You watch, from your hiding place, as the Wagon touches down. The shell of the vessel opens up with a hiss. A Drone unloads boxes of food and supplies.

Raf gives you the signal to go... but you spot an angry-looking Downsider running towards Althea — his appearance could disrupt your mission!

Turn to 37 to confront the Downsider.
Turn to 80 to stick to the plan.

All four of you made it! Three bashed and dented insect-like vehicles crawl away from the water processing plant… and grind to a halt. You're all out of fuel. You stagger out of your vehicles and step on to warm, clean sand. The sun beats down. Cade jumps around, punching the air. Of course — he's never seen the sky!

Dotted about the landscape are strange, featureless buildings. They look like vast, black glass pebbles that have dropped out of the sky. There are no roads, but some silver bubbles are moving slowly across the sky. You shade your eyes from the sun and look up at the nearest gleaming, black tower. Through the smoky glass you can make out the words 'World Council'.

'Follow me,' says the Doctor, and he passes into the building, as simply as if he was stepping into the shade of a tree. You all follow him into its cool interior.

Flashing his psychic paper around and using a lot of important-sounding words, the Doctor soon commands an audience with the World Council. The Upsider Councillors wear white robes. They look strange, but in a different way to Cade. The sunlight has blinded their eyes and toughened their skin.

You watch with admiration as the Doctor introduces Cade to the assembled Councillors and puts forward his case. From his pocket, he produces the spider-like device that Cade planted on the anti-gravity unit down below. He passes it around the room for the Councillors to explore with their fingers. He explains how Cade could have used his invention to block the anti-gravity field and bring the Up Side crashing down — but he did not.

Then the Doctor impresses the Councillors with talk of Cade's experiments with transport systems and energy sources. He encourages the Upsiders to see that Cade is an inventive, passionate and creative human being — every bit their equal.

As the Doctor leaves the Council Chamber, the Upsiders have gathered around Cade and are listening intently as he explains his ideas and ideals.

By the time you emerge from the World Council building, the blazing sun has recharged the vehicle's energy cells. With the fuel cells recharged, you can pilot Cade's vehicles back to the Down Side.

Pilot the mantis over to 101.

You're the first to dive through the flap and slide down the laundry chute — a metal slide that was once used to carry used bed sheets to the hospital laundry.

Apart from anything else, it looks like it might be fun! It's a bumpy ride but hopefully you're going to end up somewhere clean and tidy.

No such luck. You drop out of the bottom of the chute into a pile of stinking waste. Someone has been throwing rubbish down it — and turned the old laundry into a dump.

Ooof! The Doctor drops out of the chute and lands on top of you. You're just recovering from that when Martha lands on top of you both.

'Thanks for the soft landing, guys!' chuckles Martha.

'Everyone all right?' asks the Doctor, brushing himself down. You're shaken but unhurt and so you nod. 'Then let's get out of here!'

You leave the hospital via the nearest door.

Turn to 43.

70 The Doctor has an idea.

'Up here, we're above the force field that guards the anti-gravity unit. So there's a chance we could slip into the anti-gravity stream,' says the Doctor, obviously excited, 'and bounce on it — all the way to the Up Side! What do you think, Akemi?'

'I've never tried that before,' he says. And then he grins. 'But it sounds like it could be a blast!'

'A blast?' says Payton. 'This isn't some new extreme sport!'

'Is there another way up?' asks Martha. Akemi explains that you could wait for the next food drop from the Up Side and sneak on-board a Drone Wagon, but you'd be running the risk of dealing with a fresh wave of Drones.

You're running out of time. Are you prepared to make the leap of faith? Turn to 39. Would you rather wait for the food drop? Turn to 86.

As the Doctor wanders off to look around the fair, you introduce yourself to the young woman. She tells you her name is Teah. Her skin is pale and her eyes are large and dark. 'I hope our appearance here didn't frighten you,' she says. 'And I'm sorry about your fall.'

As she speaks, Teah moves her hands and it's hard not to stare at the silvery white strands of fine hair that float from the sleeves of her dress. Also, pausing between words, she flicks out her tongue as though she might be tasting the air between you.

Teah explains that she and her boyfriend, Akemi, were meeting Payton, the man in the robes, to talk about getting married. But Akemi is from the Up Side, while she is part of a Downsider colony. Their relationship is forbidden and so they meet in the hall of mirrors in secret.

You ask Teah about the Up Side but, before you can find out any more, the Doctor calls out to you.

Turn to 75.

The Doctor walks slowly down the stairs. Because the staircase spirals down to the left, it's hard to see him ahead. You stay as close as possible, without walking into him.

The stairs are uneven and you trail your hand along the wall to help you keep your balance. As you move downwards you can feel it getting damp and slimy.

You rub your hand on your sleeve to get rid of the wetness. When you put your hand back against the wall, something moves away from beneath your fingertips. You want to scream but you manage to keep it in.

The Doctor stops and asks you if you are OK.

If you want to carry on down the stairs, turn to 74. If you'd rather not go down any further and you'd like to head back up to the chapel and find Martha, turn to 33.

The floor tilts underneath you like the floor in a fairground fun house. The next thing you know you're looking up at the domed, copper-coloured ceiling of the strange room. Black tubes and pipes hang down.

You must have fallen over. You get up and brush yourself down, embarrassed. Martha asks you if you're OK and you nod. You ask the Doctor what just happened.

'I'm not sure exactly,' he says. 'Which button did you press?'

You point to the green one.

The Doctor puts on a pair of spectacles and peers over the control panel. There's a pause while you wonder if he's going to slap his forehead and say, "Not the green one!" But he doesn't. He says, 'Fair enough!' And, 'I haven't pressed that one for yonks! I can't even remember what it does!'

'We'd better find out then, eh?' chuckles Martha, and she opens the door of the TARDIS...

Turn to 5.

74 You can't see anything at all. You listen hard. The scratching and hissing that you heard before is now much closer. The Doctor whispers to you that he is going to put on a light. As soon as the Doctor flicks on his torch, the hissing becomes louder.

The stone floor and the damp walls are crawling with milky white cockroaches, each one at least as big as a dinner plate. You take a step backwards and something crunches and wriggles under your foot.

You look up. The ceiling is squirming with giant, translucent grubs, some of which hang down on gloopy threads. One of the grubs peels off the ceiling and drops, heavily, on to your shoulder. You let out a loud cry of disgust as you flick it off.

'Let's get out of here,' says the Doctor. But you don't hear him because you're already scrambling back up the stairs. The Doctor follows you back out through the chapel.

Turn to 2.

The Doctor has discovered a force field. You ask him how he found it.

'Using a very sophisticated method,' laughs the Doctor. 'I walked into it!'

You reach out and touch the invisible force field. It feels slightly squashy, like when you push the positive ends of two magnets together. Payton explains that the force field is protecting the A.G.U.

'What's an A.G.U.?' Martha wants to know.

'An anti-gravity unit. They support the Up Side,' explains Teah. 'The new surface. Where Akemi lives.'

'How did you get down from there?' the Doctor asks. Akemi is about to answer when you hear a clacking sound, a bit like wooden castanets.

'My colony!' gasps Teah. 'They're looking for me!' Teah seems to disappear, while Payton and Akemi lead the Doctor and Martha in different directions.

To go with Martha and Akemi, turn to 30. To follow the Doctor and Payton, turn to 16.

The door opens without a squeak and the man doesn't look around. All three of you go through the door… into a broom cupboard! It's dark, and smells damp and mouldy. Martha stands alongside a stinking mop.

'Ew!' she says. 'I don't think that's been used in a long time.'

Peering back around the door you can see the security guard. He is approached by a gang of people – they're all dressed in black and their faces are hidden by hoods. You expect the security guard to menace the scavengers but the opposite happens.

The gang speak in strange, rattling voices. 'Go away! You don't belong here.'

The ragged bunch of people pick up rubbish and throw it at the guard. He raises his weapon, but it doesn't stop the gang. The guard doesn't use the weapon – he just hurries away.

To try and catch up with the guard, turn to 7. To follow the group, turn to 21.

'I know another way out of this building,' says the guard. 'You can follow me, or put yourself at the mercy of that colony.'

You think about the hooded figures swarming around the entrance to the security building and choose to follow the guard.

He tips a table up on to its end and climbs on to it so he can reach the ceiling. He slides a ceiling panel over to one side and hoists himself up into the roof space and offers you and Martha a hand up. The Doctor joins you as you crawl towards an air vent. The guard swings it to one side and you hop out to the ground below.

'It's always a good idea to have an escape route planned,' explains the guard. 'You never know when a colony of Downsiders are going to show up.'

'What's a Downsider?' Martha wants to know. The security guard laughs at Martha's ignorance. How can she not know about the Downsiders? She says, 'Let's just say we don't really fit in here.'

'Tell me about it!' the guard laughs again. 'Downsiders live on the old surface. The Upsiders send them food parcels and energy cells but they're unruly. Troublemakers.'

You wonder what he means by 'old surface'.

'Down here, in the dark,' says the guard. 'The sky is mostly blocked out by the Up Side. Anti-gravity technology was supposed to be the answer to all our housing problems. But only the rich can afford it.'

'While the old surface of the Earth is left to rot,' says the Doctor. 'I'm the Doctor, by the way.'

'A doctor! Perfect! Then you might be able to help me with my mission,' says the guard. 'My name is Rafal — you can call me Raf.'

As you follow Raf away from the deserted car park, you allow yourself one last look around to the hospital and the security building… just in time to see several hooded figures disappear into the darkness…

Go to 97.

You wait with Martha, watching as the Doctor explores the edge of the force field using his sonic screwdriver.

'This is an anti-gravity unit,' the Doctor shouts across to you, 'or an A.G.U. It's well protected, because it's holding up something big — something big enough to block out the sky.'

The Doctor stops as the sonic screwdriver unlocks a maintenance 'door' in the force field. 'Ah-ha! I've found an access point, so now to take a closer look at the...'

The Doctor stops talking and races across to the A.G.U. He starts working at it, with his sonic screwdriver. Martha wants to know what it is, but the Doctor is too frantic to answer. He yanks a small spider-like device away from the A.G.U.

'That was a bit too close for comfort,' shouts the Doctor. Before you can ask him what he has found, you are suddenly aware that something very large is looming over your shoulder...

Turn to 60.

You tap on the window. Nothing happens for a few, long seconds and then you hear the coughing again.

You shout through the window, trying to reassure whoever is there that you mean no harm. You say that you only want to help the child. Then, you hear a scuffling...

And a pale face with hollow black eyes appears at the window! You scream! The face screams! And the Doctor rocks backwards as you recoil away from the window.

'Hey! Careful!' says the Doctor, holding you steady. You can see now that the pale face belongs to a woman. She pulls the hood of her black robes over her head. She picks up her child and runs out of the room.

You climb down and tell the Doctor what you saw. You race round to the front of the salon to find the mother and child are safe — and being consoled by Martha. Good job she was waiting round the front!

Turn to 47.

You deactivate the first Drone in the way Raf showed you — with a swift kick to the back of the right knee joint. It's a glitch that not many people know about. It loosens all the Drone's joints and it drops to the floor like a puppet that has had its strings cut.

The second Drone attempts to escape in the Wagon. The Doctor switches on the sunlamp and swings it in the direction of the Wagon. The amplified UV rays block the Wagon's navigational system and force it to make an emergency crash landing!

Raf deactivates the second Drone and you jump up into the cab of the cockroach-like Wagon. Martha, the Doctor, Althea and Cal get in the back and the shiny black shell snaps shut around them. You are just about to take off when you realise the stray Downsider is clinging to the outside of the Wagon!

Althea cries out. 'Andreas!' You delay your escape by a few seconds. It is worth it to see Althea reunited with her husband — and Andreas reunited with his son!

Turn to 98.

81 As you leave the lighthouse, a new sensation hits you. A pungent, fishy smell.

'Urgh,' says Martha. 'The sea looks... ill.'

The air is humid and still. It's not really like being by the sea at all. But crossing it is the only obvious way over to the mainland. There is a small motor boat with a pair of oars in the bottom.

The distance to the mainland is only a couple of hundred metres — the journey should not be too difficult.

As you get into the boat, the Doctor examines the motor. He notes that it is powered by a solar cell that is, 'unsurprisingly dead'.

Do you offer to row the boat? Turn to 66. Or do you leave it to the Doctor and Martha? Turn to 44.

You knock on the door and a female voice says, 'Go away! Leave us alone!'

You say that you mean no harm and that you want to help the child. You listen for a reply, but all you hear is a scuffling behind the door and then silence. Raf joins you at the door and tries to force it open. There's something up against it. He tells you to stand clear and starts kicking at the door.

The Doctor grabs Raf's arm, saying, 'Steady on!'

But Raf has already kicked open the door, pushing away the chair that was propped behind it. You run into the room. There are three tanning beds and some personal belongings... and the window is wide open.

You run to the window and look outside. There's quite a drop below, but the mother and child are safe and are being consoled by Martha. Good job Martha was round the back!

Turn to 47.

83 You feel sad to relinquish control of your vehicle but, frankly, you don't believe you could make it out to the water fields on your own. You squeeze into the cab of the Doctor's grub-like vehicle. You lose sight of the others as the Doctor steers the grub into the sea. After only a few seconds, the ground drops away beneath the wheels of your vehicle and your progress becomes slow.

You see a flash of tentacles in the dark water around you! A giant squid, brought up to the surface of the water because of the darkness, is pulling you down! The Doctor urges you to take control of the grub as he solves the problem. He uses the sonic screwdriver to charge a dead energy cell and electrify the surface of the grub.

As you power the vehicle out of the water and up the side of a steel pipe, the squid gets a shock and lets you go with a disgusting plop! You are relieved to make it up the pipes and through a portal to the Up Side.

Turn to 68.

84 You ignore the guard's request to leave the building with him and, surprisingly, he shrugs and says, 'OK. But there's a colony of Downsiders on the warpath, and they'll smell you out, even in amongst all this rubbish.'

What does he mean, 'colony of Downsiders'? But it's too late to ask as he's already left the room. You glance over at the monitors. The hooded figures are now showing up on the second monitor — they are entering the building!

You hurry out of the room, just in time to see the guard disappearing through a door in the opposite direction to the entrance. You can hear a horrible rattling and hissing coming from the reception area, so you follow the guard through the door and into a paper-strewn office. The filing cabinets have been ransacked and the desks turned upside down.

The Doctor locks the door behind you. It looks like you're trapped in here with the security guard.

Turn to 77.

You observe the security guard opening doors along the corridor and sweeping each room with a hand-held console.

'A thermal imaging device,' explains the Doctor. 'He must be looking for someone — and he's leaving no hiding place unchecked.'

It's only a matter of time before... he spots you! He turns around. You can't see his eyes because of the large goggles. He strides in your direction, raising his weapon. You can't help but turn away.

'Stop!' shouts the guard in a commanding voice. 'I order you to stop!'

There's no way you can get back to the TARDIS without him catching up with you. The Doctor uses the sonic screwdriver to open the door of a lift. Martha is pushing open a flap in the wall.

'A laundry chute,' says Martha. 'Come on! Let's go!'

To dive down the laundry chute, turn to 69. To hop into the lift, turn to 55.

You say you'd rather wait for the 'food drop' — whatever that is. And whatever these 'Drones' are — they can't be as terrifying as jumping off the top of a rollercoaster. The Doctor looks a bit disappointed, but Payton agrees with you.

'No one has ever tried it before,' he says. 'It's too dangerous.'

'I think it could work,' says Akemi. 'What about you, Teah?'

'I don't mind,' she says. 'As long as we stay together.'

Suddenly, an electric blue laser bolt bounces off the rails at your feet. You all turn around to see a vehicle hovering in the air, less than a hundred metres away. It looks like a giant black metal cockroach — with laser cannons.

Another blast of laser fire leaves you unharmed but shakes the rollercoaster, knocking you off balance. You stumble. The Doctor tries to help you, but you're out of reach... Your whole body leans over the edge of the rollercoaster and you fall...

Upwards!

Turn to 49.

You follow Martha as she looks for another way up the rollercoaster. Quite soon, you come across a maintenance ladder, running up the inside of the structure.

'Bingo!' whispers Martha. 'I knew there had to be another way up.'

The Downsiders are circling around you – so Martha starts climbing and you follow close behind. As you scramble up the old and long-disused ladder, you can hear it creaking and groaning.

Bits of rust drop down into your eyes and hair. You want to brush them away but you dare not let go of the ladder for long enough to do so. Perhaps this is why Akemi climbed up the structure of the rollercoaster instead...

The ladder starts to shake. You look down. The Downsiders are grouped around the base of the maintenance ladder. But, for some reason, they're not climbing up after you... Instead, they're ripping the ladder away from the wooden frame of the rollercoaster!

You shout up to Martha. She looks down and sees what's happening. You can see the panic on her face. You have to do something – and quick!

Keeping your weight on your left foot, and holding on tight with your hands, you kick down on the ladder below with your right foot. A couple of good kicks and you kick out a rusted rung of the ladder. It drops down into the Downsiders below, sending them scattering.

A few more kicks and the rusty ladder beneath you begins to break away. Now the Downsiders can pull the bottom of it right off — but you can continue your journey upwards without fear...

How you're going to get back down again, however, is another matter...

You climb onwards — up to the highest point of the rollercoaster, the hissing and clacking sounds of the Downsiders fading away below.

Turn to 17.

The Doctor strides off to explore the fair and you approach the man dressed in white. He yanks off a pair of mirror-lensed goggles. His narrow, sloping eyes have white, milky irises. He smiles warmly and introduces himself to you as Akemi. He shakes your hand with a firm grip.

Akemi explains that he is here to meet Teah, his girlfriend. He puts his arm around the waist of the pale girl, and you see that Teah looks as frail and delicate as Akemi is strong and hearty. She looks up at him with unusually large, dark eyes.

They are in love and were hoping their friend Payton, the older man in the robes, would be able to help them marry. But there's a big problem... Akemi is from the Up Side and Teah is a Downsider. You're about to ask Akemi what he means, when the Doctor calls out to you. You rush over to find out what he's discovered.

Turn to 75.

Some humming and flickering white lights illuminate the abandoned hall of mirrors. You push through the turnstile and it goes round easily as though it has been used recently. You enter the hall of mirrors.

As you step forward, a ghostly figure looms out of the darkness in front of you — but it's just your reflection. You shiver, but Martha doesn't seem phased.

'If I touch the wall with one hand and keep walking,' says Martha confidently, 'I'll eventually find my way through the maze.'

Martha touches the mirrored wall in front of you with her left hand, and her reflection reaches out and touches her back. She sets off to the right, trailing her left hand along the wall.

To follow her into the hall of mirrors, turn to 34. To take your own path through the mirrors, turn to 11.

You follow the Doctor as he moves down the aisle of the old chapel. You stay close to him and, when he stops abruptly, you walk smack into his back.

'Steady on!' says the Doctor. And then, 'A locked door — how tempting!'

Using his sonic screwdriver, the Doctor unlocks the wooden door and heaves it open. Stone stairs curve down into pitch-blackness.

The Doctor heads towards the stairwell and stands at the top, listening. You hold your breath and concentrate on listening, too. You can hear scratching — like someone rubbing a pan scrub over a metal surface — and, on top of that, a faint hissing. It all seems to be coming from down the stairwell.

Do you follow the Doctor down the stairs? Turn to 72. Or do you want to rejoin Martha at the entrance to the chapel? Turn to 33.

'I was hoping that a marriage between Akemi and Teah might bring the two Sides together,' says Payton. He's about to say more when he spots something — a Downsider, just ahead of you, in the shadows. His head is cocked to one side, listening. He flicks out his tongue tasting the air. All you can do is stand still and hope he doesn't hear you. Or smell you.

You hear a creaking sound, like a tree branch bending in the wind. A big sign on the top of the helter-skelter comes crashing down. The Downsider runs away... and the Doctor slides down the helter-skelter on his coat-tails. He shoots off the end, landing on his feet.

'All the fun of the fair, eh?' he says, brightly. He claps his hands together, creating a little puff of dust and you laugh with relief. 'I've spotted Martha,' says the Doctor. 'She's with Teah and Akemi... heading that way.' And he points up the old rollercoaster.

Turn to 26.

You close your eyes and take a deep breath. You open your eyes... and let go of the ladder!

You drop on to the track. It is slippery, but you find your footing. It certainly feels a lot safer than clinging on to that rusty old ladder. You call up to the Doctor, and down to Payton, and encourage them to follow your example.

They do as you say, taking their time and testing each section of the ladder. The Doctor observes that the Downsiders don't seem to be following you.

'They are afraid of what may come down, if they venture up,' Payton explains.

You are about to ask him what they might have to be afraid of, when you feel a hand on your shoulder. You spin round... and you are relieved to see a grinning Martha.

'We can follow the track to the top of the coaster,' says Martha. 'Akemi and Teah are waiting for us there. Come on!'

Turn to 17.

The Doctor uses the sonic screwdriver to unlock the door. The inside of the abandoned security building buzzes with low-level, emergency lighting.

Passing through a distinctly unwelcoming reception area, you walk down a corridor and enter a room lined with CCTV monitors. Some of the screens are broken and all of them are blank. There's no sound, except for the scurrying of rats, disappearing into cracks in the walls.

The Doctor punches a few numbers into a control panel. Nothing happens, so he has a go at the panel with his sonic screwdriver. That does the trick! Two monitors burst into life — the first shows the black box on the bank by the car park, the second shows the entrance to the security building.

On the first monitor, you see some hooded figures. They circle, widely, around the black box and head in the direction of the security building! You move to exit the room but the security guard from the hospital blocks your way!

'Come with me,' he orders.

To obey him, turn to 77. To resist, turn to 84.

Cade pilots the mantis, the Doctor climbs inside some wheeled thing that looks like a giant grub and Martha takes control of a relatively delicate, but still pretty heavy-duty, dragonfly-like vehicle. Your locust-like transport looks pretty cool in comparison!

All the vehicles move surprisingly quickly across land. And so, like some bizarre, fuming, insect day carnival parade, you make your way up the coast — leaving the harbour and the lighthouse far behind.

All four vehicles line up on the headland. The water fields — thick pipes, with maintenance platforms, that rise out of the stagnant sea up into the darkness above — lie about 500 metres out to sea. You talk with your companions, over your headset, about what to do next.

You are given a choice — risk jumping out to the water fields in your locust-like vehicle or join the Doctor in the grub.

To risk jumping, turn to 6. To join the Doctor, turn to 83.

Raf dives towards the dark-eyed Downsider but you block him.

'Althea!' he says.

'Andreas!' says Althea, reaching across to give him a big hug.

'Shush!' says Raf — partly because he doesn't want you to be discovered and partly because he is embarrassed that he was just about to stun Althea's husband.

'How is my son?' Andreas wants to know.

'Hanging in there,' smiles Martha, holding up Cal for him to see.

You wonder how Andreas and Althea became separated. For the rest of the journey, Andreas tells their story in a hushed voice. He explains how he and Althea could see that Cal was different and special. They realised he was important to someone on the Up Side when the Drones came looking for them. Andreas managed to divert the Drones but, in doing so, lost touch with Althea and Cal. He's so happy to see them again.

You feel the Drone Wagon touching down...

Turn to 98.

You leave the stinking beach and walk up a worn stone staircase up on to the headland. No one speaks and you suspect everyone feels the same way. Whatever has been happening here on Earth, it has been very, very bad.

You walk for a while through the abandoned harbour. All the buildings are dark and decaying like ancient monuments. A bunch of empty roads come together towards the dock and cross over in a network of flyovers.

You walk through an underpass and emerge into a pedestrian area underneath the silent roads. With no one around, and all these smooth concrete surfaces, you can't help but think this would be the perfect place to skateboard.

In the middle of the pedestrian zone is a black, rubber-coated box — it looks a bit like a car battery, only the size of a car itself.

To examine the box, go to 57. To hang back, go to 38.

As you walk along the dark, empty street, you ask Raf if he is an Upsider or a Downsider.

He cheerfully explains to you that he was born on the Up Side, but his family was banished to the Down Side for breaking the strict codes of conduct — such as keeping children indoors at all times. Now he's working for a progressive party of Upsiders, whose aim is to bring down parts of the Up Side and reunite both Sides.

You ask him why he carries a weapon, if he comes in peace. He explains that being a friend of both sides makes everyone see him as a threat. The weapon is just a piece of junk, long since broken.

'You mentioned a mission?' says the Doctor.

'Ah, yes,' Raf explains. 'It's not just Downsiders that are getting sick — the Upsiders aren't faring much better. Without these lenses, I can't see at all.' He lifts up his mirror-lensed goggles. His eyes are small and milky white.

Raf explains that humans on both Sides are changing to cope with their different living conditions — but they are not evolving quickly enough. Humankind is dying out.

His mission is to find a particular child — the great grandchild many times over of the President of the Up Side and a Downsider Rebel. The child needs to be located and protected. Raf believes that child's genes might be the key to saving the human race from extinction.

You exchange a look with Martha — could the fate of humankind be down to one child? It seems far-fetched. 'But,' says the Doctor, 'if we can save one person's life, our time here will not be wasted.'

You wonder where to start looking.

'If you had a child, starved of sunlight,' wonders Martha, 'where would you take him?'

'How about here?' says the Doctor, stopping outside a tanning salon.

To enter through the front, turn to 62.
To sneak around the back, turn to 56.

You ready yourselves for a fight on the Up Side. Both you and Martha are prepared to deactivate any attacking Drones. Raf adjusts his mirror-lensed goggles, turning a dial on the side. Even the Doctor is twizzling the sonic screwdriver around in his hand, just in case...

Andreas is carrying his child, still wrapped in the Doctor's jacket to protect him from the sun's rays. Neither Andreas nor Althea, let alone Cal, has ever seen the sky before. But none of you are prepared for what awaits you... the last thing you imagined is...

Nothing.

The Up Side is a desert, silent and still. The back of the Wagon pops open and you hop out on to the warm yellow sand. You have to shield your eyes from the sun, beating down. Althea and Andreas can't resist taking a look at the sky. The harsh light makes them cry out in pain and cover their eyes with their hoods.

Dotted around are smooth, curved buildings that look as though they are made from black glass. There's one white building. You guess that this might be the hospital.

You walk towards the white building. Turn to 100.

'Oh, they're very important,' says the Doctor. 'The President of the Up Side... and her First Man.'

'How did you know that?' says Akemi.

'Let's just say we met once before,' the Doctor smiles, 'in the future.'

Akemi looks understandably confused. Martha laughs. 'You mean — you knew who Akemi's parents were all along?' she says to the Doctor. 'You knew he was some sort of... Prince Charming for world peace?'

Now Akemi laughs, but the Doctor's busy with his sonic screwdriver. 'From up here, I think I can lower the intensity of the anti-gravity field in an area small enough to let us slip back to the Down Side, but not big enough to cause any damage to the Up Side,' he says. 'OK, that's it! Come on, you two! Hurry up!'

And so, before you know it, you've said goodbye to Akemi and you drop back down into the darkness...

Fall back down to 45.

A white glass, lozenge-shaped building, with no visible doors or windows, stands ahead of you. It looks like a huge, half-sucked cough sweet that has dropped out of the brilliantly blue sky.

Dotted on the horizon are other solitary buildings, all of them are smooth and black and featureless. No roads connect any of the buildings. Nothing moves. The Up Side seems like an immaculately clean, barren and lonely place.

A sudden burst of activity draws your attention. A pair of nurses passes through the milky white glass wall of the hospital. There must be some sort of doorway there, but you can't see it. The nurses just sort of melt into view like figures stepping out of a fog.

They are dressed in immaculate white robes and the same kind of mirror-lensed goggles as Raf. A hot breeze ruffles your hair and shakes the dirt from your clothes. You suddenly feel very self-conscious about your appearance.

The nurses rush to the aid of Althea and Andreas, who are both swooning in the heat. Raf reassures them that no harm will come to them. No attempt is made to separate Cal from his parents. The last time you see Cal, he is being carried away into the shade of the hospital. You can see his face. He is looking up at the sky... and smiling.

This is all you can take in before you, too, feel a bit woozy. The Doctor can see you look a bit wobbly. He grabs a waiting wheelchair and helps you into the cool interior of the hospital...

The hospital on the Up Side is the opposite of the place where you arrived. It is clean, ultra-modern and dazzlingly white. A few minutes inside, where it's cooler, and you feel restored. You hardly have time to take it all in before the Doctor tells you it's time to go home.

Turn to 65.

You leave Cade's extraordinary vehicles in his workshop and make your way, on foot, back down to the beach. You walk through the dark, picking your way through the piles of rotten rubbish and dead sea life.

The Doctor tells you that, after his presentation, the World Council agreed to work with Cade and lead a peaceful unification programme between the Upsiders and the Downsiders.

With the human race split into two different Sides everyone was getting sick. Too much sun, or no sun at all. Isolated living in sterile glass homes, or running around in colonies inventing things from centuries of waste. Both sides were struggling to evolve quick enough to keep up with the unnatural change.

'Bringing the two Sides together will be a new age of enlightenment,' chuckles Martha.

The motor boat is where you left it, near the beginning of your adventure. You drag it down to the scummy water's edge and clamber inside. You hope the sonic screwdriver has enough power to charge the energy cell and get you back to the lighthouse – where the TARDIS waits for you.

You are chugging across the still and sickening sea when you remember something. When you first stepped inside the TARDIS, you were running away from something…

But then you see something that makes you think that, so long as the Doctor's around, everything will turn out alright.

Because, above you, a crack is slowly appearing in the Up Side! While it is still held in place by the anti-gravity units, Cade has begun dismantling some of the plates that form the Up Side.

Ahead of you, bright sunlight begins to stream down across the sea for the first time in years. And, behind you, up on the headland — shadowy figures with pale faces are lining up to see the new dawn.

THE END